THE FAIRY DOLL

Mary Ransom

Copyright © 2024 Mary Ransom
All rights reserved

Just for you.

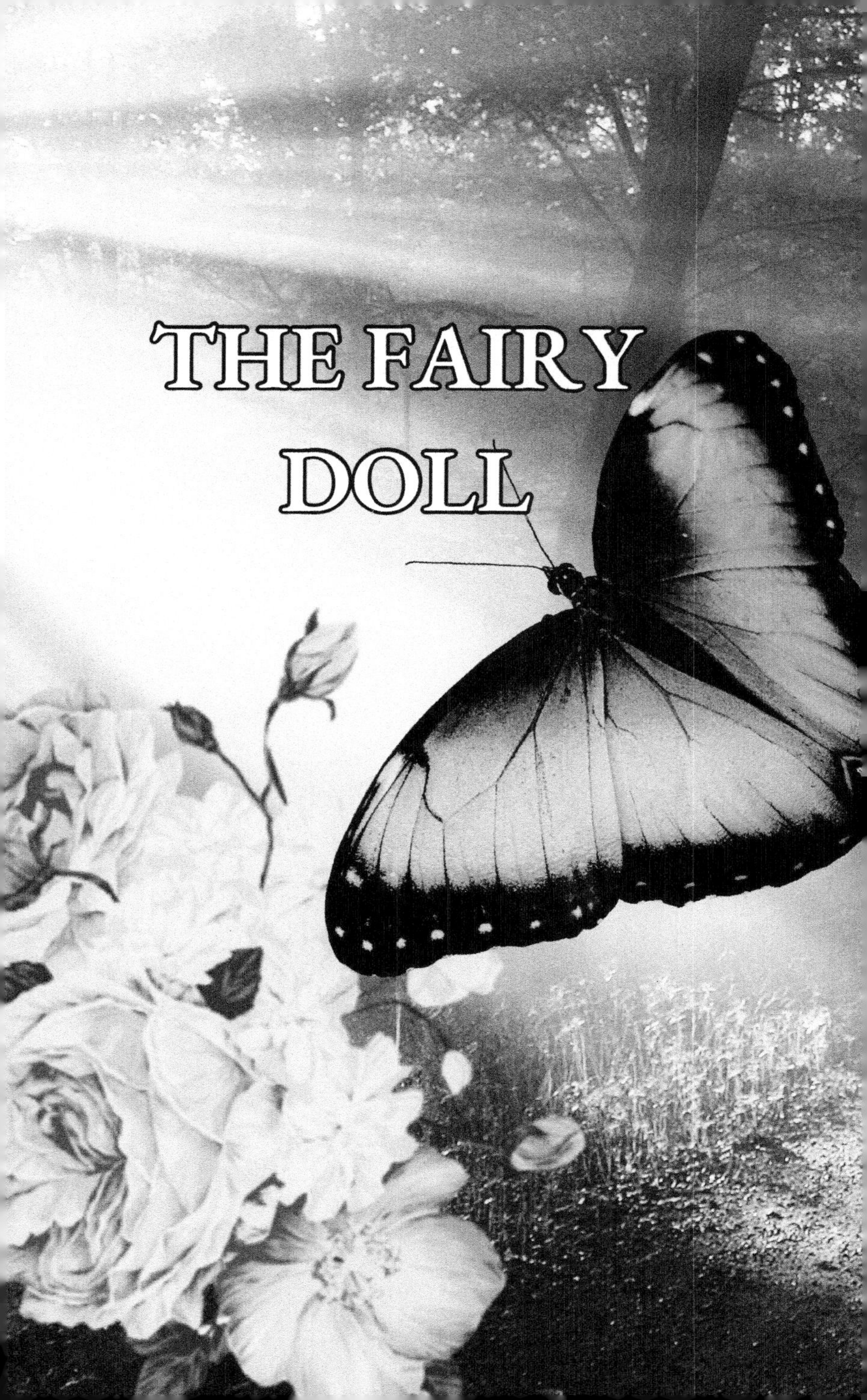
THE FAIRY
DOLL

CONTENTS

Introduction..i

Chapter One: Broken Dreams............................1

Chapter Two: Modern Technology..................8

Chapter Three: The Feathered Doll.............14

Chapter Four: Tantrums and Terrors..........21

Chapter Five: Music to my Ears....................26

Chapter Six: Lost and Found............................31

Chapter Seven: The Fairy Doll's Army.........36

Introduction

When Pandora's Box
was opened,
all the evils of the world
were released.

But did you know
that all of the evils
were dolls?

Chapter One
Broken Dreams

Pandora choked as her A.I Hunter doll fell through the cracks in her treehouse and got wedged between the broken floorboards.

She quickly brushed the splinters and dust from her black, curly hair and waited for an apology, from the knee-high doll, but the garden fell silent.

"So much for my relaxing day off!" moaned Pandora. "What are you doing up there, anyway? Certainly not hunting for our runaway Pandora's Box Dolls, like you promised." she hissed.

For once, the argumentative little Hunter doll said nothing, which only made Pandora more angry. The doll's spindly legs just dangled back at her, four feet above the teen's face.

Pandora sat up from her grey and olive beach towel. It was draped across the soft grass to mimic a day at the beach, only now it resembled a day at a building site.

She reached up and tugged the doll's right leg, convinced that one of the doll's tacky accessories had become stuck in the opening, but the doll didn't move.

THE FAIRY DOLL

Pandora groaned. It was Hunter's...

ROUND,
   TIGHTLY STUFFED,
     COTTON FILLED,
       COMPUTER CHIPPED,
        RAG DOLL BELLY

...that anchored her in place,

like an egg in a cup!

"You greedy doll! You've broken my treehouse!" Pandora shouted at the swaying pair of pink and purple camouflage socks. "How am I going to get you out of there now?"

There was a long silence while Pandora waited for a response, but only the faint rustling of paper could be heard. She backed away, hoping to catch a glimpse of Hunter's sulking top half, only her body was still obscured by the base of the treehouse.

Finally, Pandora could take no more. She ran to the rope ladder and began to climb. The wooden rungs hung clumsily from the main tree trunk and they creaked under her weight, yet nothing could stop her.

Full of determination, she reached the tree branch at

record speed, crawled through the Labrador-sized doorway and locked eyes with the sulking doll. Pandora's oak brown eyes fixed to Hunter's coal black eyeballs like a magnet.

Hunter froze. Her mouth was visibly full and her jaw was still chewing, behind her solid, porcelain face mask.

"Jellies..." mumbled Hunter.

Pandora snatched the bag of sweets from the doll's smooth, plastic fingers and waved them out in front of her.

"You watched me bake a fresh batch of my famous, homemade flapjacks this morning!" Pandora snapped. "And now you're up here, eating junk food, instead of waiting for pudding?"

Hunter didn't take her eyes off the white, sweetie bag for a second. Then with her arms outstretched, like a battering ram, she lunged at Pandora's hand and reclaimed her secret treasure.

Pandora shook her head as the doll unplugged her bottom from the splintered hole and fell face first into the cabin's soft, teal rug.

"You could get out of there all along? What a fool you are!" Pandora moaned.

She removed a zip-lock bag of flapjacks, from the

pouch on her hoodie, and put it to her nose before unzipping an inch at the corner. The vapours exploded from the opening faster than the evil dolls had escaped the Pandora's Box, thought Pandora, smiling.

To the girl's delight, Hunter tilted her head towards the rich, oaty smell, just as she had hoped. Then with lightning speed, Pandora pulled the bag away again.

"Well, now you're not getting a single one of these, Hunter! I'm going to share them with some other doll, who actually appreciates flavour, instead of you..." Pandora huffed and then she pointed a shiny fingernail at Hunter, just to double the impact of her threat.

"...NOT SOME GOOSE-GUZZLING POD
that
SUCKS IN FOOD LIKE A BLACK HOLE
and then asks for
MORE!"

Hunter shrugged, scooped up the bag and forced a fistful of sweets into her mouth. It was a sickening sight to watch her scoff the lot through the tight, black slit between her fixed, porcelain lips. Pandora quickly turned away.

"What's the rush, Panda?" Hunter spluttered. She

swallowed hard before continuing, "I had everything I needed up here, and besides, I'm not hunting down any evil dolls for you today...or babysitting your ugly Pandora's Box! It's my day off."

Pandora climbed down from the treehouse and lay back on the fresh, daisy-filled grass of her family home. Her Dad was inside the living room, watching the news and posting updates to Pandora's phone every five seconds. She sighed. Not one day passed without him either blaming himself for the devastation that the escapee dolls had caused, or pushing Pandora to catch more dolls.

She thought about her late Mum too and how she would have been instantly forgiven by her kind, loving nature. The sun burned down onto her face as she turned back to the grumpy Hunter doll.

"Maybe you've forgotten that it's *my* day off too? And I don't want to spend it lounging on my lawn, staring up at your knickers, all day!" Pandora huffed.

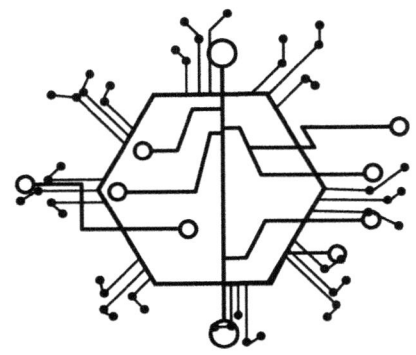

Chapter Two
Modern Technology

Hunter joined Pandora, sunning herself beside the line of daffodils in the back garden. She sprawled out over the grass like a sea star.

Pandora took this moment, of temporary silence, to close her eyes and relax a little. She breathed in deeply,

**smelling the bark of the trees,
the crispy rays of sunshine
hitting her tanned skin**
and... **FRUITY JELLY SWEETS.**

THE FAIRY DOLL

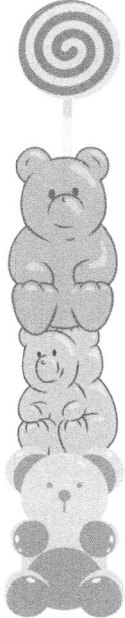

She turned towards Hunter, who was now balancing a tower of treats on her forehead.

"Oh, I've had enough of this!" fumed Pandora. She reached for her phone, "I'm turning on the Doll App! I'd rather spend the day fighting evil dolls than babysitting one!"

Hunter bolted upright. Her black, beady eyes focused instantly on the screen, almost bulging with excitement.

"Please, Panda, can we hunt down the Fairy Doll together?" Hunter begged, "She'd look so pretty in my dolls house, next to the other dolls I've put on display."

"I thought that you didn't want to capture any dolls today," said Pandora, smiling, "or were your tantrums this morning just my overactive imagination?"

"What tantrums? I don't remember any of that strike business and besides, we've already got our picnic packed." giggled Hunter.

She reached for the syrup stuffed slices of warm, heavenly goodness that lay on Pandora's lap, but they were speedily pulled out of her grasp.

"Oh, no you don't. These flapjacks are my favourite treats and I'm putting them in my bag...

...for myself."

snapped Pandora and she stuffed the homemade wedges into her beach bag before going back to her phone.

A tiny head with golden hair poked in between Pandora and the her doll's app. She moved her mobile to the left and then back to the right but couldn't shake the peeping pest.

"I can't type with your head in my face! Move it or lose it!" cried Pandora, only the doll turned her head one hundred and eighty degrees to stare daggers back at her.

Pandora dropped the phone and it buzzed back a beautiful image of an idyllic wild spring situated in deep, unspoilt woodland.

"Wales, UK." beamed Pandora, "That's what I need. A real holiday! We can stay at a charming bed and breakfast place, have a relaxing walk through the quiet woods and then hunt down the Fairy Doll on our way back home."

"And eat Welsh rarebit!" Hunter screeched, interrupting Pandora's ramblings with such passion that she almost triggered a 'glitch' headache.

The doll giggled as Pandora wrapped her hands around Hunter's mouth to stop the high pitched din but couldn't get past her porcelain mask.

"It's the world's finest cheese on toast." Hunter added, softly.

With a quick tap of her finger, Pandora accepted the challenge to capture the Fairy Doll via her app and waited for the portal's co-ordinates to paradise.

"Shouldn't you say goodbye to Mr Pandora's Dad, first?" asked Hunter, spoiling the mood.

"I've already said goodbye, silly. Look, I've been talking to him on live stream for the past twenty minutes." explained Pandora and she waved at the tiny human on her screen.

"Are you kidding, Panda? Now he's going to blame me for breaking that treehouse!" cried Hunter, "And after all the work I did on editing my photograph up there."

"What photograph?" replied Pandora.

"The selfie I took, when I was stuck between the floorboards, of course! I pasted a picture of your face

over mine so that he would think that you broke it instead. Oh, I just hate modern technology!" Hunter groaned.

The doll's words flashed around Pandora's skull faster than an Olympian cyclist.

"You artificially ignorant, doll.

YOU ARE MODERN TECHNOLOGY!

Now wedge these Fairy Doll co-ordinates in your stuffed head and make me a portal to Wales!" roared Pandora. "We're going on holiday!"

Chapter Three
The Feathered Doll

"Please, give me a sign!" begged Pandora, casting a pitiful silhouette of a lost clown, falling to her knees before yet another Welsh road sign.

A guttural pronunciation of the foreign words rumbled from the Hunter Doll's internal speakers, but as Pandora turned to congratulate her on translating the sign, she realised it was just the greedy doll's stomach rumbling.

Pandora groaned, Hunter wasn't the only hungry nuisance in the area. She stood up quickly as her trembling body was mobbed by a large group of ducks. They had followed them down the empty roads for the past twenty minutes or so.

Pandora cleared her throat. "Well, this is all your fault, Hunter! You were supposed to drop us off within a mile of the Fairy Doll's co-ordinates, not in the...

MIDDLE OF NOWHERE!"

"But, Panda...the Fairy Doll **LIVES** in the middle of nowhere. So, I didn't really get the address wrong. I followed the app, like you told me to." reasoned Hunter before blowing her a raspberry.

"Then,

**WHERE'S THE FAIRY DOLL'S SPRING?
THE CHARMING WELSH INN?
THE RELAXING WOODLAND WALK?
THE...THE CHEESE ON TOAST?"**

asked Pandora, attempting not to stutter as her mouth turned crisp in the cold, foggy air.

"Please, don't mention food, Panda! We've been running around looking for a hotel for hours! Can't we just teleport home and then come back tomorrow?" Hunter begged.

The doll patted her round, cotton belly, inspecting it for wrinkles in case she had lost weight. She panicked for a moment, when finding a dimple, until Pandora informed her that it was just the indent of her belly button.

Pandora sighed. "I guess you're right." she said, feeling the weight of her first defeat. But it couldn't be helped. "Just don't tell Dad that we got lost. He'll only worry and I don't want him involved in all this."

Hunter nodded but didn't say a word, possibly because she was cold. Or maybe, out of fear that Pandora would change her mind and make her stay just to punish her for not being able to connect to an internet map service.

Exhausted, Pandora reached for her phone, only her fingers ceased up in the cold winds. She juggled the gadget in mid-air before it was snatched out of her grasp by a hungry, white duck.

There was an instant of flapping wings, intense quacking and the pecking of several jealous beaks, as the flock of ducks assumed that one had been fed. A loud squeal rang out from Hunter as her tiny body disappeared in the middle of the rioting birds.

Pandora reached out her hand. Hunter went to hold her but slipped. There was a bang of metal on the concrete road, startling the ducks and causing them to dash into the fog ahead. Pandora left the doll on the ground and ran after the ducks. She was chasing her mobile phone, following the angry quacking sounds until suddenly they went silent.

Pandora ran through the fog before stopping dead in her tracks. She stared ahead through a thick, ancient forest that had appeared out of the mist like magic.

The phone was gone, forever, Pandora was convinced of it. She retreated to where Hunter lay covered with both white and speckled feathers.

"Please tell me that you can get us home without the Doll App!" The words rushed out of Pandora's mouth on fire, as though they were attached to the base of a rocket ship.

"I think..." started Hunter, throwing an invisible lifeline at Pandora before finishing her sentence "...I hear a spring! Quick, it's inside that

ancient,

    creepy,

        enchanted,

            little forest!"

THE FAIRY DOLL

cheered Hunter and she ran in-between Pandora's legs towards the creaking woodland.

Pandora tried to stop Hunter from running into the gloom but the doll dived like a goalie facing a penalty kick, leaving her alone on the road.

The sun quickly descended behind the treetops, but try as she might, Pandora couldn't hear any kind of dripping or spring-like sounds. There was nowhere to run to, no matter what Hunter had said. They were surely doomed.

She tucked her hands into the sleeves of her hoodie and contemplated the harsh choices ahead of her.

- spend the night alone on the roadside

or

- spend the night in one of Wales' natural treehouses

With a deep breath, she peered into the dense forest and took a step forward. After all, if she left now, she was sure to catch up with Hunter, easily. A wicked smile stretched across her chilled cheeks. Then she could really let her have it!

Chapter Four
Tantrums and Terrors

Pandora groaned as her calf muscles stretched like badly tuned violin strings. Her quest to catch the Fairy Doll was now second to her struggle to reconnect with Hunter, in the Welsh forest. But that didn't stop the pinched cheek doll from storming even further ahead. She had the legs of a cheetah and only stopped to occasionally click her fingers for Pandora to follow.

An hour came and went. Pandora groaned again. She was convinced that not even a competent A.I device could distinguish a bubbling spring from within

the stew of deafening calls that now surrounded her.

The nocturnal creatures filled the air with chirps, cries and growling but no one knew what sounds a Fairy Doll could make. Not even Hunter, or she would have caught her already.

This was getting silly, she thought. Of course, her mind was still filled with some hope, although rather small, but as the darkness rolled in, even that was diminishing.

Pandora hoped that her eyes would stay open for long enough to find the Fairy Doll.

Pandora hoped that Hunter wasn't leading her in ridiculously long circles and

Pandora hoped for a great deal of other things whilst trailing Hunter's shadow.

But an hour come and went, until the shoes on her feet rubbed like sandpaper on her heels.

Hunter hadn't said a word in over twenty minutes, but made herself known by falling over various roots, fallen logs and stumps along the trail. Pandora listened for the thump of Hunter's knees as she fell over each obstacle in the darkness. It baffled her. She didn't think that any hunter could be so clumsy as to fall over eight stationary logs on the trail, but Hunter had squashed her theory, bringing her close to mental breakdown.

"Hunter, just face the facts! You have no idea where you're going, do you?" Pandora yelled into the night.

A million sounds growled, scuttled and flapped back back at her, but none of them were from Hunter. Pandora boxed in her shoulders. She wanted to go home and snuggle up in a warm throw on the sofa but without her phone, they were stranded.

No phone meant no app and no app meant no co-ordinates to use to get home. Pandora lost her footing on something slippery and fell face down on what must have been the only fully exposed slime hole for miles.

She cried in desperation and although Hunter raced back to her side and offered a tiny hand to help pull her up, Pandora pushed her away again.

In all honesty, Pandora was cross and embarrassed at doing the one thing she had moaned at Hunter for doing the past hour, that was, being clumsy.

"I don't need your creepy eyes judging me, okay? I just slipped on..." Pandora looked down to examine her trainer, only she was hit first by the awful smell of whatever was stuck to the tread, "...POOP!"

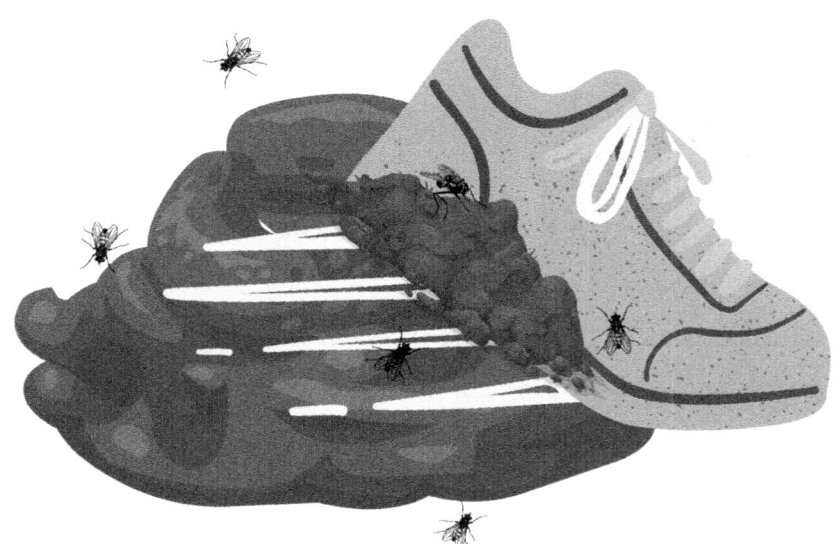

Hunter chose this exact moment to have another temper tantrum and stormed off ahead, upset at Pandora for shouting at her kindness. But Pandora was far too angry with the state of her shoes to apologise, and instead bellowed a callous,

"you're supposed to be guiding us to water, not dung!"

in Hunter's general direction.

Suddenly a crash of thunder tore through the air, stopping Pandora dead with eyes like an owl's. She leaned forward and listened again. Strangely, from the shadows emerged a small, glowing rock that tumbled towards her like a bowling ball. She jumped in sheer terror.

"Hunter, what's green and purple and rolls?" Pandora shouted into the darkness, ahead, hoping that the grumpy doll would know what this odd little thunder ball was.

There was a shout from the distance. "I'm not in the mood for jokes, Panda! You don't need my creepy eyes judging you, remember?"

Chapter Five
Music to my Ears

In the depths of Pandora's soul, was the horrifying belief that she was caught up in the middle of an earthquake. She leapt behind the smooth bark of a nearby Beech tree and waited. But the small, rolling rock was the only thing that moved on the forest floor.

With a fallen twig, Pandora tapped the ball lightly and to her surprise, a great rumbling tore through the trees once again. The thunderous noise echoed throughout the area and beyond, yet this time, she was was not afraid.

Pandora knelt down to observe the miraculous event of watching a tiny lime coloured leg emerge from this shell-like material. Within moments, the leg was followed by a skinny arm and then a fragile wing.

A tear trickled down Pandora's nose as she stared at the magical creature before her. There was no doubt in her mind that this was the Fairy Doll, freshly transformed into her final shapeshifting form.

Pandora glowed inside because she had found the doll all by herself. She didn't need that poor excuse for an A.I bot, Hunter, for anything. Except maybe to praise her amazing discovery.

"Hunter!" she yelled whilst squinting into the night air, "You can come back now because I've found the Fairy Doll. She's beautiful!"

Pandora inspected the doll. There was a stained glass effect on the fairy's wings, that would have suited a tissue-paper butterfly from an art project. But perhaps the most impressive thing about the woodland creature was sat upon her left arm.

Getting a little closer, Pandora saw that fused to the fairy's bone was a stringed harp, in the shape of a medieval shield. The Fairy Doll reached for the tiny instrument, with her right hand, and began to play a melody.

The rough, protein shell fractured quickly all around the fairy's body, setting off a dozen after quakes that silenced the wild animals. Pandora's heart melted. The Fairy Doll stared lovingly up at her with glossy, blue button eyes. She resembled a shop brought fairy tale creature, only this one was real.

Every instinct that told Pandora to run was muzzled by those enchanted orbs of sapphire coloured eyes. They were so bright, even in the low light of dusk, that they lit up the surrounding area and the night appeared as day. This humanoid nature spirit had the long, flowing hair of Pegasus. White and silky to the touch. Her flesh was of the green Imp, but she wore loose, delicate threads, similar to the veins on an ivy leaf and her eyelashes were laced with gold and glitter.

In the magical fairy's glow, Pandora was overjoyed. She stumbled back but to her amazement, there was another egg laying beside her foot. Pandora scanned the pathway only to see hundreds of fairy eggs littering the forest like fallen leaves.

THE FAIRY DOLL

The Fairy Doll smiled peacefully at Pandora, as though accepting the girl as her carer. She then opened her plump, apple red lips and spat a sickly puddle of black tar onto the foliage, barely an inch from Pandora's foot.

"Uh, yuck!" Pandora bleated and she jumped back about a meter from the goo, almost losing a shoe in her haste to stay clean.

The mass of trembling eggs boomed a tsunami soundwave throughout the forest. Pandora's hands darted to protect her ears but her eyes suffered a greater shock. She watched as the black puddle expanded to double it's size and mercilessly dissolved every root, leaf and piece of soil that it touched.

Pandora stumbled again. This time in a blind panic and screamed the only two words that really meant anything to her. Which happened to be:

HUNTER
and
ACID

Scarecrow-clawed branches slashed at Pandora's arms and legs as she fought past the twisted realm of overgrown trees to escape being charred. Only, each time she glanced back, the vile doll was still there. Her wings beat tirelessly in predatory pursuit and hundreds more Fairy Dolls were only just awakening to join in.

These dolls weren't transforming, Pandora screamed in the vastness of her silent mind, they were clones. She wrapped her bare fingers around the solid wedge of an overhanging sycamore branch and pulled her sweating heap of a body up from the forest floor. There she waited, breathing cold air through her puffed sleeves to disguise the sounds of her whimpering.

Chapter Six
Lost and Found

The morning sun peeped over the treetops and flooded the woodland like syrup on a crumpet. It's warm, gentle rays cloaked Pandora's shoulders with much needed comfort after being flopped over a Sycamore tree branch for eight hours, straight. But the Fairy Doll's clones were long gone and her head still dreamed of that cosy Welsh bed and breakfast that she desperately longed for.

Pandora stirred awake in the peaceful sunlight and opened her blurry eyes in sheer wonder at how she had managed to climb so high up in complete darkness.

The tree was a wicker basket of hardwood security and held Pandora's weight well. But at the very top, the leaves had thinned out and there was precious little bark to hold on to. The lonely teen swayed in the wind.

"So, I ended up sleeping in a tree after all?" whispered Pandora, before slapping her dry tongue to the roof of it's lair and attempting to find Hunter's night time stash of orange juice, only she remembered that the doll wasn't there.

"Hunter! Are you down there?" Pandora cried to the empty woodland, below. No one answered.

Slowly her scrambled memory pieced back together until the puzzle as to why Hunter had stormed off, earlier, returned.

"Hunter? I'm so sorry that I was mean to you! Please come back!" she yelled into the undergrowth but the forest remained eerily silent. "Fine then! Stay lost, you unforgiving, little coward!" she snapped.

It was heart-breaking to imagine how Hunter must have found the original Fairy Doll's spring by now and was probably lounging happily on the surface of the water in an inflatable, doughnut accessory of hers.

"Yeah, you just enjoy yourself!" she roared in delirious rage whilst trying not to fall to her grave.

It was a strange feeling, she thought, to be staring down at a death-defying drop, over a forest of black tar and disintegrated earth. The ground resembled holey cheese. She watched the morning mist form shapes on the horizon as she climbed down the mammoth tree, a step at a time. The air got clearer with each second that passed.

The icy blue fingers of Pandora's right hand loosened their grip on the tree branch. She gasped and her blood pumped faster. Beneath her was a beautiful, natural spring. She had been sleeping above it all night.

Careful to avoid any dead or brittle branches in her way, Pandora descended quicker then before. Fear plastered her face with a sea of worry lines and wrinkles, but within ten minutes she had managed to feed her body down through the mesh of

tangled leaves, offshoots and rough, gritted bark.

It kind of resembled the fibres in a patchy, knitted blanket, only, no where near as soft. Pandora found that out the hard way, spending most of her time falling from one branch to the next instead of climbing.

Finally the charred ground was within sight and she jumped safely to the ground with a thud.

"Hunter! Where are you?" Pandora cried, collapsing in the dirt.

An instant seat formed beneath her bottom in the soft mud and masked her face with dread. The cold, squelching feeling that glued her jeans to the earth was bad enough but she had to also nurse a scraped thumb from her night in the canopy.

The sun rose higher and the shadows that had caked the woodland in gloom had now retreated to the underworld and Pandora could see the beauty of an isolated, natural spring stretched out all around her.

At last she could breath easy. The endless hours of walking in circles in the dark had paid off and just resting in this beautifully enchanted clearing balanced her mind, body and soul. Around her grew fens and mosses and an abundance of wildlife buzzed, jumped and nested up beside her.

Suddenly a snapping sound, like that of a twig being broken in two, scared off the squirrels. Pandora smiled at the familiar sound of Hunter's leg falling over another branch, and span around on her bottom to apologise. But the hypnotising glare of two solid blue eyes met her instead and filled Pandora with dread.

Standing behind her, barely a meter away, was a six foot tall green and white image of doom. The Original Fairy Doll, and Pandora was in her domain.

Chapter Seven
The Fairy Doll's Army

Pandora stared up at the Fairy Doll who towered over her, at over six feet tall. Her brain dispatched a speedy delivery of fuel injected adrenaline to her leg muscles. Yet there was no where to go. She was surrounded by miniature fairy clones who beat their wings as though they were whipping a tornado into creation.

She found it hard to believe that the same beautiful fairies, that had tried desperately to coat her in acid the previous day, were again preying on her at the spring.

Pandora ran in the opposite direction to the giant Fairy Doll however, her long, thin arms reached out for her regardless, like creeping vines up a wall. Pandora jumped over a pile of dissolving tar and ran to the other side of the spring but the fairies followed her.

One-by-one, the enchanted army opened their mouths and flew straight towards her, spitting poisonous chemicals directly at her body. Pandora dodged again but slipped on small piece of plastic litter and fell awkwardly on her right ankle. She tried to move but it was twisted and painful.

The original Fairy Doll lifted her hand and her clones stopped their attacks. They lined out a path for the Fairy Doll, as though on parade to show off their loyalty to a beloved ruler.

Pandora held her ankle tightly and tried to crawl away, only the Original Fairy Doll walked over to her, like a human would, rather than using her glittery wings.

The Fairy Doll grinned, exposing a mouth full of serrated teeth. It chased Pandora's body another few feet as the girl scrambled to get away. But suddenly Pandora's back hit hard against a large tree and she had nowhere left to turn. The Fairy Doll then opened her blood red lips and pounced down in ambushed delight. Only, Hunter's grin was wider. The little doll leapt out from behind the old oak tree and held onto the giant Fairy's imp-like body, holding nothing but a few vines and reeds.

Pandora watched as Hunter proceeded to fold the doll's paper-thin wings around it's own monstrous mouth, like an envelope.

"Quick Panda, catch!" yelled Hunter and she threw Pandora's lost mobile phone into her lap. "You have no idea what I had to do to get that back! But these vines won't hold her for long. Open the app and I'll get you out of here!" screamed Hunter.

"But Hunter, what about you?" cried Pandora, only the doll just shook her head.

"If I go with you, the whole world will be covered in this acid! Just promise me that you'll look after my dolls house, Panda. My dolls accessories are now yours." said Hunter, losing her sparkle and coming close to tears.

Pandora typed her address into the Pandora's Box Doll App and the co-ordinates of her home flashed on the screen.

"I'm ready, if you are." whispered Pandora, picking up the small zip lock bag that she had tripped on and recognising it as her half-empty flapjack bag.

The Hunter Doll held the Fairy tightly, it's clones were too afraid to spit acid at their queen but her grip was loosening fast.

"Most of them went to the ducks, Panda, I didn't eat them, I..." Hunter's words were drowned out by the fizzing of the purple portal that the doll had summoned for Pandora's getaway. "Bye-bye, Panda. I've always loved you."

Pandora pulled herself up on her knees and threw a flapjack from the bag at the Fairy Doll. All at once, a great flock of ducks ran in from all angles of the woodland, fighting to get a nibble or a crumb. The quacking mob pushed the giant Doll into the portal instead of her and Hunter's mouth fell open as she fell to the floor.

The many fairy clones flew in after her, their beautiful faces carved with concern for their chosen one.

"What are you doing?

YOU STUPID HUMAN! YOU'VE JUST DESTROYED THE WORLD! DON'T YOU KNOW WHAT YOU'VE DONE?"

thundered Hunter above the sound of angry ducks.

The spring filled up with even more of her tears. But Pandora just lay back on the grass. She held up the phone towards Hunter's wet face mask and smiled.

"Well, I didn't say WHERE at home I made that portal to." said Pandora with a wink. "I just showed you the co-ordinates to the inside of the Pandora's Box!" she laughed.

Hunter's skinny arms gave way and she fell on her face, exhausted in the mud. Pandora laughed with the ducks, still squabbling for food.

The sun burned down onto her face as she turned back to the grumpy Hunter doll.

"So much for my relaxing day off! But at least you're not still holding onto that giant Fairy Doll! I don't want to stare up at your knickers, all day!" Pandora huffed.

THE END

No dolls were harmed in the making of this book

Printed in Great Britain
by Amazon